Friends and Foes

COLUMBIA PICTURES PRESENTS A MARVEL ENTERPRISES/LAURA ZISKIN PRODUCTION
TOBEY MAGUIRE 'SPIDER-MAN 2' KIRSTEN DUNST JAMES FRANCO ALFRED MOLINA ROSEMARY HARRIS DONNA MURPHY
MUSIC BY DANNY ELFMAN EXECUTIVE PRODUCERS STAN LEE KEVIN FEIGE EXECUTIVE PRODUCER JOSEPH M. CARACCIOLO BASED ON THE MARVEL COMIC BOOK BY STAN LEE AND STEVE DITKO
SCREEN STORY BY DAVID KOEPP AND ALFRED GOUGH & MILES MILLAR SCREENPLAY BY ALVIN SARGENT PRODUCED BY LAURA ZISKIN AVI ARAD DIRECTED BY SAM RAIMI

MARVEL   SPIDER-MAN CHARACTER ® & © 2004 MARVEL CHARACTERS, INC. ALL RIGHTS RESERVED.   **sony.com/Spider-Man**   **COLUMBIA PICTURES** © 2004 COLUMBIA PICTURES INDUSTRIES, INC. ALL RIGHTS RESERVED.

Friends and Foes

Written by Michael Teitelbaum

Based on the Motion Picture

Screenplay by Alvin Sargent

**Screen Story by Alfred Gough &
Miles Millar and Michael Chabon**

**Based on the Marvel Comic Book by
Stan Lee and Steve Ditko**

HarperFestival®
A Division of HarperCollins*Publishers*

Introduction

A red-and-blue streak flashes above the New York City skyline as police sirens scream in the street below. A dark shadow moves silently among the city's rooftops, swift and unseen. Somewhere a crime has been committed, and the police need a hand. The amazing Spider-Man swings into action.

When trouble strikes, Spider-Man is there to lend a hand . . . or a web, as the case may be. Whether the situation involves an attack by a supervillain, a bank robbery, or helpless people

trapped inside a burning building, Spider-Man is first on the scene.

He is referred to by many nicknames—the webbed wonder, Spidey, web-head, wall-crawler, and web-swinger, to name a few. But who is this mysterious, misunderstood, masked figure?

In this book you will meet the man behind the mask and come to know his friends, his family, his allies, and his enemies. All of your favorite characters from *Spider-Man 2* are here. So what are you waiting for? Swing into action with your friendly neighborhood Spider-Man!

Peter Parker

ALWAYS ON THE RUN

Nothing ever comes easy for Peter Parker. His life is a constant juggling act. He is forced to balance his studies as a college student at the city university, a part-time job, and his freelance job as a photographer for the *Daily Bugle* newspaper. With so many things to do and so many places to be, Peter's many priorities overlap, forcing him to always be late or not show up at all.

Peter is number one when it comes to

taking Spider-Man photos. In fact, he is the only photographer in the city who can manage to get a shot of the webbed crusader. Peter sells his Spider-Man photos exclusively to the editor of the *Daily Bugle*, J. Jonah Jameson.

Jameson doesn't know why Peter is the only photographer who can get photos of Spider-Man. But that is because he doesn't know that Peter *is* Spider-Man. In order to manage the hard-to-get shots, Peter uses his webbing to attach his camera to a high

building ledge, and then sets up his camera to automatically snap shots of himself—as Spider-Man—in action. The money
he makes from the photos helps Peter to
pay the rent, but even on a good day,
money is *always* tight.

Peter also looks out for his widowed aunt
May. She lives alone in Queens, and Peter
tries to get there as often as he can, but
with all of his responsibilities that is not
always as often as he would like.

He also just happens to be on call 24/7
as the wall-crawling, web-slinging hero
known as the amazing Spider-Man!

A DIFFICULT BEGINNING

Peter's life was tough almost from the
beginning. Orphaned at a very young age,
Peter went to live with his aunt May and
uncle Ben, which was a rare lucky break in

an unlucky life. The frightened child was suddenly living with two people he hardly knew. But Uncle Ben and Aunt May raised Peter with love and support. They were as caring and giving as any parents could have been.

Still, things were not easy for Peter. He was a shy boy, and kept mostly to his books and chemistry set. He became an honor student in science, one of the brightest kids at Midtown High School in Queens, New York.

One seemingly ordinary day, Peter's life changed forever. While attending a demonstration on genetically engineered spiders on a school-sponsored field trip, Peter Parker was bitten by one of the spiders. He underwent an astonishing transformation, acquiring the powers of the spider and becoming Spider-Man.

Having his spider-powers was a gift and a curse for Peter. How could he balance all of his responsibilities? Most of the time, Spider-Man had to be in one place, while Peter Parker needed to be in another.

PETER TAKES MANHATTAN

After high school, Peter left Queens. He lived in a Manhattan loft with his best friend, Harry Osborn, while he started taking college classes at the university. But

the loft was just temporary, and Peter soon moved into his own studio apartment. It was a very small place, without much privacy, but since Peter was hardly ever there, it was OK.

His landlord, Mr. Ditkovitch, was always after Peter for the rent money (after all, as the landlord, that was his job). When Peter would come home after a long day of either school, work, or being Spider-Man, without fail, Mr. Ditkovitch was waiting for Peter's rent money.

In between his jobs and school, the juggling act that became Peter's life also included spending time with his elderly aunt May.

Since the death of Uncle Ben, Peter tried to visit his beloved aunt, who now lived alone, as often as he could. And naturally, he missed his uncle tremendously.

With all he had to do, Peter was having trouble getting to his university classes on time. His favorite professor, Dr. Connors, was greatly disappointed in Peter. Dr. Connors was a stickler for punctuality and felt that Peter was not taking his studies seriously. But Dr. Connors had no way of knowing that with the amount of time Peter spent as Spider-Man, rescuing the citizens of New York City, plus juggling all of his other obligations, Peter had trouble balancing those responsibilities. And Peter could not tell his favorite professor the reason he was always late, either. He just had to hope that Dr. Connors would tolerate his tardiness because he did indeed love school. He hoped Dr. Connors would ignore the fact that almost all of his research papers were turned in late.

AROUND TOWN

While Spider-Man (as you will later learn) flew around town by swinging on his webbing, Peter was resigned to travel on the ground. He owned a motorbike that got him from home to school, school to work, sometimes work to work, then eventually home.

Peter's motorbike was not the most glamorous mode of transportation. It was not as cool as a motorcycle, but then again, he was a college student who could

not afford a motorcycle. But when it came to zipping though the alleys of Manhattan, and skipping over the bridge to visit Aunt May in Queens, Peter was content with his yellow motorbike.

PETER IN A NUTSHELL

And, of course, Peter was still madly in love with Mary Jane Watson, the object of his affections since she moved next door to Aunt May and Uncle Ben's home when Peter was six. Even though his feelings seemed unrequited, Peter never gave up hope that he and Mary Jane would some-day be together.

Balancing all of his duties as Peter Parker with his responsibilities as Spider-Man kept Peter constantly on the move. But this intelligent young man always took his responsibilities very seriously.

Spider-Man

SPIDER BITE

Spider-Man came to be through an incidental, accidental occurrence. While on a school field trip, senior high school student Peter Parker was busily snapping photographs. It seemed to be a perfect day—Peter was on assignment from the school newspaper, visiting the coolest research lab in the entire city, and Mary Jane just happened to be on the trip.

Suddenly, a tiny, genetically engineered spider dropped from the ceiling and landed

softly on the back of the young man's hand.
Without Peter even knowing that the spider was there, it bit him, changing his life forever.

In an instant, Peter felt the stabbing pain of the spider bite, followed by a wave of dizziness. The pain failed to subside, and Peter felt lousy the rest of the day. Upon arriving home from the lab's demonstration, Peter went right to his room, where he fell into a fitful, fevered sleep.

When Peter woke up the next morning, everything about him was different. The skinny kid suddenly had muscles. His vision, which had always required glasses, was now perfect. He felt a strength coursing through his veins unlike anything he had ever felt.

He soon discovered that he could stick to walls and climb up the sides of buildings. He could leap huge distances, like from rooftop to rooftop. In addition to great strength, Peter now had agility beyond that of an Olympic gymnast. He also found that he could sense when danger was about to strike *before* it happened. It was all unbelievable and indescribable to Peter.

And there was also the webbing that shot from his wrists, allowing Peter to swing from building to building. He had acquired the powers of the spider that had bitten him. What would he now do with these awesome abilities?

WITH GREAT POWER COMES GREAT RESPONSIBILITY

At the time, it seemed like a good idea for Peter to use his newfound powers to make a few bucks. Putting on a makeshift costume, Peter answered a challenge for anyone who could stay in the ring with an undefeated wrestler. Peter won the match easily.

Following his victory, Peter failed to stop an escaping thief, figuring that catching crooks was not his responsibility. Then came the event that changed his life as much as the spider bite.

The thief that Peter had let get away then murdered Uncle Ben. Peter could

have easily used his powers to stop the thief, but he chose not to. Obviously, he had no way of knowing that his decision would result in such a horrible occurrence, but it was then that Peter learned the lesson that would guide his actions from that day forward: With great power comes great responsibility.

A HERO COMES ALONG

Spider-Man was born. Peter made a promise to himself, and to the memory of his uncle, that he would devote himself to fighting crime. He would stop villains and help the people of New York in any way he could. The formerly shy and awkward student was now the city's greatest hero.

Spider-Man decided to always wear a mask and to keep his true identity a secret. He feared that if his enemies knew who he really was, they would try to hurt those he loved the most.

Unfortunately, not everyone in New York believed that Spider-Man was a hero. J. Jonah Jameson, publisher of the *Daily Bugle* newspaper, constantly ran headlines accusing Spider-Man of being a menace— even an outright criminal! These headlines were usually accompanied by a photo of

Spider-Man taken by Peter Parker. Recently, Peter decided not to sell his photos of Spider-Man to the *Daily Bugle* (or any other paper for that matter). He didn't like the way J. Jonah Jameson had been treating Spider-Man in the headlines.

THE SPIDER SKINNY

Imagine what a spider as big as a person could do. That represents just some of the powers of Spider-Man. Just like a spider has the ability to lift many times its own weight, Spider-Man can lift almost ten tons. He can also bend iron bars with his hands, punch a hole right through a brick wall, and lift a bus off the ground. And that is before lunch!

But Spider-Man is not just about brute strength. He combines his amazing might with incredible agility and speed. His ability to think fast and move even faster allows the webbed wonder to perform amazing acrobatic maneuvers. He can leap the length of an entire city block or jump five stories straight up. He can spin around flagpoles, somersault over a gang of attackers, and even dodge bullets.

Aiding Spider-Man's lightning-quick reflexes is his spider sense. This danger-detecting ability starts as a tingling sensation in the back of his skull, growing more intense as the danger draws nearer. Spider-Man's spider sense goes off if a gun is pointed at him, or if someone attempts to attack him from behind. Having spider sense is like having a built-in radar system. Something can be falling from the sky or about to explode near Spider-Man, but his spider sense will warn him in time to safely avoid the danger. Because of this, it is impossible for his enemies to sneak up on the wall-crawler.

This unique ability, combined with his strength and agility, aids Spider-Man in battle. It guides him as he web-swings among the rooftops of the city, always leading him to a safe spot.

WEB-TASTIC

In addition to being a quick and convenient way to get around, Spider-Man's wall-crawling power also affords him the element of surprise. It allows him to silently and swiftly sneak up (or down) on an enemy.

Perhaps Spider-Man's handiest power is his ability to shoot webbing. Spider-Man's webs have many uses. He can fire a thin strand over a long distance, creating a rope for swinging from place to place. He can also fire his webbing in a sticky liquid form that is more powerful than the strongest glue. This sticky webbing is good for holding a criminal in place until the police arrive.

Spider-Man can also weave his webbing into a parachute, a safety net, or a fire-proof shield. Sometimes he uses his webbing to create a backpack to hold his street clothes while battling bad guys.

INSIDE THE SUIT

Spider-Man's costume is a tight-fitting bodysuit made out of a synthetic stretch fabric, specially designed to fit beneath his regular clothes. Creating Spider-Man's mask took a great deal of Peter Parker's scientific ingenuity. The big white patches that cover his eyes are actually special one-way lenses. They allow him to see out but prevent anyone from seeing in.

With all of his amazing abilities, the one thing that Spider-Man cannot control is the mixed feelings with which the public views him. At times he is called a hero, and his strong sense of responsibility drives him forward. Other times, he is accused of being a menace, or a danger to the city.

But he always recalls the promise he made to himself after Uncle Ben's death: to use his awesome powers to protect the innocent and stop those that would harm them. Then Spider-Man is once again web-swinging through the concrete canyons of New York City.

Aunt May

WITH LOVE, ALWAYS

Aunt May has been like a loving mother to Peter for as long as he can remember. She has always been there for him no matter what. She worried about him when he was late coming home, fretted when he didn't finish a meal, and wanted only the best for her nephew. Intelligent and insightful, Aunt May could tell that Peter loved Mary Jane Watson even before Peter himself knew.

Though Peter lives in Manhattan now, he visits Aunt May at her house in Queens as

often as possible. That is, when his duties as Spider-Man allow him to. Peter works very hard to protect his secret from Aunt May and to make sure that his alter ego does not put her into harm's way. But sometimes things happen that are out of even Spider-Man's control.

He was horrified when one of his enemies—the Green Goblin—figured out that Spider-Man was Peter Parker. Armed with that knowledge, the Green Goblin attacked Aunt May to get to Peter/Spider-Man.

Fortunately, the situation worked out all

right, but Peter hopes that no other villain learns of his secret again. Because of the situation with the Green Goblin, Peter has a constant and nagging fear that Aunt May might be in danger from Spider-Man's enemies.

WELCOME HOME

Aunt May, on the other hand, is always ready with a warm smile, a helpful hand, or

a freshly baked pie. She enjoys Peter's visits and is there to welcome him home each and every visit. As expected, she continues her role as a very important part of Peter's life.

In the two years since Uncle Ben's death, things have gotten tougher for Aunt May. She lives on a fixed income and sometimes has trouble paying her mortgage. But because Peter has so much on his mind, Aunt May does not wish to burden her nephew with her troubles. She knows that it will all work out in the end,

Still, what Peter and his aunt lack in money, they make up for in love. Uncle Ben's death only drew them closer. No matter what happens, Peter will always look after her, and Aunt May will always be there for Peter, offering unconditional devotion and support.

Mary Jane Watson

THE GIRL NEXT DOOR

Mary Jane Watson has come a long way, even in just the past few years. Things had been tough for her growing up, but she is finally starting to realize her long-held dream of becoming an actress.

Mary Jane's good fortune started when she was given a modeling job for a catalog. The photographer was so struck by her beauty that she ended up on billboards throughout the city, as the face of the Emma Rose Parfumerie.

Next, Mary Jane got a job playing the role of Cecily Cardew in an off-Broadway production of *The Importance of Being Earnest*. She was wonderful in the role, and it made Mary Jane very happy that her friends Harry Osborn and Aunt May had both come to see the play. Conversely, she was very disappointed that Peter hadn't yet found the time to do the same.

LOVE COMES KNOCKING

Mary Jane always liked Peter Parker. Even going back to when they were just kids, he was gentle and kind to her, and he was always there for her during tough times. Mary Jane held a special place in her heart for the boy next door, Peter Parker. Sometimes she wondered if Peter felt the same way, and if there could ever be more than a friendship between them, but Peter

always seemed too busy. It seemed like a hopeless cause.

Mary Jane started dating a handsome young astronaut named John Jameson (who just happened to be the son of the *Daily Bugle* publisher J. Jonah Jameson— Peter's boss at his freelance job). Mary Jane liked John very much, and the feeling was mutual from John. Mary Jane was thrilled that John wasn't distracted and distant like Peter always seemed to be.

OCK ATTACK

One afternoon Peter and Mary Jane decided to meet for coffee. It was awkward at first, and Peter didn't know what to say—Mary Jane had been angry with him for so long.

Mary Jane wanted desperately to mend her relationship with Peter, and he felt the same way. So many positive things had happened in her life, and Mary Jane wanted to be on good terms with the one person who had always stood by her through all of the difficult times.

Then, before either of them had the chance to figure out a way to patch up their friendship, an uninvited guest tore into the café.

Peter's spider sense had picked up on the intruder. But he had no way of knowing what was about to happen.

Doc Ock launched a parked car through the café window! Bricks and debris flew everywhere, knocking Mary Jane and Peter to the ground.

Mary Jane was frightened, and as she looked to Peter for help a single thought went through her head: *How will we get out of this nightmare?*

Harry Osborn

A SILVER SPOON

Harry Osborn was born into a life of wealth and privilege. But that did not mean that he had an easy time of things, especially during the past two years.

Harry's father, Norman Osborn, died two years ago, and Harry was trying to follow in his father's footsteps as head of special projects at OsCorp, a company that Norman had built from the ground up.

What Harry didn't know was that in addition to being a brilliant businessman, his father had also been the villainous Green Goblin, an evil force who had terrorized the city. The Green Goblin died as a result of a battle with Spider-Man, but Harry didn't see what happened between the two—all Harry saw was Spider-Man returning Norman Osborn's lifeless body to his home.

FRIENDS AND ENEMIES

From the moment Spider-Man delivered Norman's corpse, Harry Osborn blamed Spider-Man for the death of his father. It can only be described as a bizarre twist of fate that Harry Osborn considered Peter Parker his best friend and Spider-Man his worst enemy! In fact, Harry sometimes became angry that Peter got close enough to Spider-Man to take his photo, but wouldn't tell Harry where Spider-Man could be found.

But Harry and Peter remained best

friends. In fact, Harry was overseeing a special project being conducted by a scientist named Dr. Otto Octavius—one of Peter's heroes. Harry knew that Peter was writing a school paper about Dr. Octavius, and he was pleased to be able to introduce Peter to the famed scientist.

Otto Octavius

HUMBLE BEGINNINGS

As a child, Otto Octavius actually had much in common with Peter Parker. He was a shy and sensitive boy, a hardworking student who always performed well in school.

During college, Otto studied science, and it was there that he met his loving wife, Rosie. Right from the start, Rosie was a great source of strength and support to him. She also helped the prodigy to understand that there is more to life than just academia.

Eventually, after years of work and determination, he became Dr. Otto Octavius, a brilliant and well-known scientist.

OCK AT OSCORP

Dr. Octavius's latest research was being funded by OsCorp under Harry Osborn's Special Projects Division. The doctor's research and experiments often called for him to work with dangerous chemicals, unstable compounds, and radioactive materials.

Because these substances were far too deadly to handle with bare hands, Dr. Octavius created a mechanical harness containing four metal arms. Using these arms, he could handle virtually any type of dangerous material safely.

Then came the fateful day when a lab accident bonded the mechanical arms Dr. Octavius had created to his body. Otto found that he could control the arms using his mind. He also discovered that the arms had a mind of their own. In fact, *they* could control *him*. The supervillain Doc Ock was born!

Who could have ever guessed that both Peter and Otto would undergo amazing transformations—one so powerfully good, the other so overwhelmingly evil—forcing the pair to become archenemies?

Doc Ock

AN OCK IS BORN

In the accident that turned Dr. Otto Octavius into Doc Ock, the mild-mannered, good-natured scientist was overtaken by the evil genius of his mechanical arms. Octavius ceased to exist and Doc Ock was unleashed on the world.

Octavius had created the harness and mechanical arms in order to work with dangerous radioactive substances. A lab accident fused the arms to his body and mind, making them as much a part of who he was as any of his natural limbs.

The arms were made of high-impact metal. They were extremely powerful, yet incredibly precise. In their normal state, each arm was about six feet long, but they could telescope, extending up to thirteen feet in length!

At the end of each arm was a pincer. These mechanical "fingers" were so strong that they had the ability to crush solid rock. Yet Doc Ock had such great control over his metal arms and pincers that they performed delicate scientific operations on material too dangerous for humans to touch.

Doc Ock used the arms in battles against Spider-Man. They were also used for traveling. Rising up on the arms as if they were giant metal legs, Doc Ock could walk great distances quickly. He also did a Spider-Man

impression, climbing up walls. But Doc Ock
did it by punching handholds into the sides
of buildings.

Doc Ock remained in constant mental
contact with his tentacles no matter
what—even when he was out cold. The
arms enjoyed the capability to protect him

from harm even if he should lose con-
sciousness.

Cunning and dangerous, this brilliant scientist became one of Spider-Man's most
dangerous foes.

47

J. Jonah Jameson

WHO'S THE BOSS?

"Where's Parker!" boomed a commanding, coarse voice, echoing throughout the halls of the *Daily Bugle* newspaper. This could mean only one thing—the *Bugle*'s publisher, J. Jonah Jameson, had arrived in the building. He wanted his best (though he would never admit it) and favorite (he would sooner choke than admit that one) freelance photographer, Peter Parker. And he wanted him *now*.

Jameson was cheap, blustery, and

grouchy, and those were his good points. But he was a newspaperman through and through. It had been said that rather than blood, J. J. had newsprint running through his veins. No one who knew him would argue that fact.

Jameson had become famous for his editorials against what he called "costumed vigilantes." The rest of the world called them heroes.

His favorite target was Spider-Man.

From the moment the web-slinger burst onto the scene, Jameson began running stories about how the costumed crusader was a menace. He accused the web-head of everything from robbery to being late when returning library books.

Jameson knew that Peter Parker brought him terrific photos, particularly shots of Spider-Man. But that information would never be shared with the freelance photographer. If a shot was worth three hundred dollars, he offered Peter one hundred.

For all his bluster and hot air, Jameson knew that he had sold a lot of newspapers since the day that Peter Parker first walked into his office and Spider-Man first began web-swinging around New York. And that made him very happy, not that he would ever admit it.

John Jameson

LIKE FATHER, LIKE SON?

John's father, J. Jonah Jameson, was very proud of him. Handsome, smart, and heroic, John Jameson was an astronaut, one of NASA's youngest space explorers.

Aside from the connection of John Jameson's father being Peter's boss at the *Bugle*, there was a second link between the two men—a more personal one.

John Jameson met Mary Jane while she was waiting tables in a diner. They hit it off immediately and started dating. John went

to see her play, and Mary Jane was always at his side during the many social events that came with being an astronaut. John and Mary Jane made a beautiful couple, and it seemed to everyone around them that they belonged together.

Everyone except Peter, that is. Peter himself had always been in love with Mary Jane. He was upset when he learned that the pair had started dating, and he felt worse when he was asked to take photographs at a party at the planetarium. At the party, Mary Jane, looking radiant in a sleek black evening dress, descended a staircase on the arm of John Jameson, handsomely attired in his air force uniform. Peter could only watch.

Betty Brant

A FRIEND AT WORK

Betty Brant was J. Jonah Jameson's secretary at the *Bugle*. Peter and Betty first met when Peter showed up at the *Daily Bugle* offices to sell Jameson photos of Spider-Man.

Betty was one of the few people who knew how to get along with the long-winded, short-tempered publisher. She let her boss rant and rave, while quietly making sure that the business of getting out a newspaper was taken care of. Betty was

the eye of the hurricane, the calm in the middle of the storm.

Once, when a homeless man came into the *Bugle* office with a great story, Jameson offered him only a hundred dollars and a bar of soap! In one of Betty's typical moments of kindness, she gave the homeless man a lot more money, money she hoped would get the man back on his feet.

Dr. Curt Connors

THE PROFESSOR

Throughout Peter's life, he has had the good fortune to have several strong role models to step into some of the roles his father would have filled.

Uncle Ben was as much a father to the boy as anyone could have been. He was there for Peter day after day. Later, Norman Osborn, impressed by Peter's scientific brilliance, took the high school student under his wing. When Peter reached college, the man he most looked up to was his science professor, Dr. Curt Connors.

Shortly after graduating from medical school, Dr. Curt Connors lost his right arm while serving as an army surgeon. He was forced to give up his work as a surgeon and so became a teacher and a researcher.

Dr. Connors was a brilliant and gentle man who loved doing scientific research. He also loved teaching. The professor got great joy from inspiring young, curious minds, and he immediately saw the potential in Peter to be a great scientist.

Because of this, Dr. Connors was frustrated by what he saw as Peter's laziness. His prized student would always be late for class and late in turning in assignments. The professor had no way of knowing that the reason for Peter's lateness and apparent lack of focus was not laziness at all—it

was his double life as Spider-Man.

Most recently, Peter was doing a paper for Dr. Connors' class, the subject of which was a "smart arms" experiment being performed by the brilliant Otto Octavius. Dr. Connors knew Dr. Octavius personally, and knew all about the smart arms experiment. He warned Peter to be sure to do his research and to get his facts straight!

Robbie Robertson and Ted Hoffman

JOURNALISTIC BOSOM BUDDIES

Robbie Robertson and Ted Hoffman worked more closely with *Daily Bugle* publisher J. Jonah Jameson than anyone else on the *Bugle*'s staff.

Ted Hoffman was a valuable employee, though Jameson often implied he wasn't. Ted kept Jameson constantly informed of changes or problems, and gave up-to-the-minute updates in the operation of putting out a big city newspaper. He also came up with ideas that Jameson took credit for. Fortunately, Ted took it in stride. It was all part of working for J. Jonah Jameson.

Joe "Robbie" Robertson was the *Bugle*'s editor-in-chief. Unlike his blustery boss, Robbie was a soft-spoken, easygoing man. He functioned as the voice of reason and compassion at the paper, and often found himself in the position of being Jameson's conscience.

Robbie had been kind to Peter Parker from the moment the young photographer

stepped foot into the chaotic offices of the *Bugle*. He recognized Peter's talent right away, and to this day, maintains his role as a buffer between Peter and Jameson.

Unlike Jameson, Robbie remains objective about Spider-Man. Jameson decided from the moment he first set eyes on Spider-Man that he was a villain. Robbie chose to give the webbed wonder the benefit of the doubt and decided to judge him on his actions. Robbie was also one of the few people at the *Bugle* who would stand up to Jameson and let the publisher know when he thought Jameson was wrong.

Postlude

A CAST OF CHARACTERS

With so many characters in *Spider-Man 2*, it is difficult to pick a favorite. And what are they up to now?

• Our hero, Peter Parker, continues his calling as Spider-Man, saving the citizens of New York City from villainous outlaws.

• Aunt May remains in Queens, always missing her beloved husband, Ben.

• Mary Jane Watson continues to shine on the stage and in Peter's heart.

• Harry Osborn is trying to make a name

for himself and get out of his father's shadow.

• Having morphed into the nefarious Doc Ock, Dr. Otto Octavius is gone forever—or is he?

• J. Jonah Jameson is as grouchy as always, never giving up on his dislike of Spider-Man and love of making his employees shudder.

• As an astronaut, John Jameson maintains his high-action lifestyle.

• Betty Brant may not work for the nicest guy in town, but she always carries herself with style and grace.

• Dr. Curt Connors is fulfilled and content, helping to develop the young minds at the city university.

• Robbie Robertson and Ted Hoffman are still on staff at the *Daily Bugle*, keeping J. J. in check and mentoring the neophyte journalists.